I Miss School

ISBN 978-1-0980-8828-6 (paperback)
ISBN 978-1-0980-8829-3 (digital)

Christian Faith Publishing, Inc.
832 Park Avenue
Meadville, PA 16335
www.christianfaithpublishing.com

Printed in the United States of America

I Miss School

Michael Marinaccio

GiaBella is a happy eight-year-old girl who loves school and now misses school very much.

GiaBella was sitting at the kitchen table eating her favorite breakfast— pancakes with strawberries, bananas, blueberries and whipped cream, which she always asked her mom to make it look like the sun.

GiaBella was getting ready for her remote learning.

GiaBella said, "Mommy, I miss school."

Her mother replied, "What is it about school that you miss?"

GiaBella didn't have to think too long, as she quickly replied, "I miss riding on the school bus with my friends."

"Riding on the school bus is so much fun. I would sit next to Eva and Antonio."

"What else do you miss about school?" her mother asked.

GiaBella said, "I miss a lot of things. I miss..."

GiaBella started thinking.

"I miss my classroom and friends."

"I miss my desk full of sparkles and my hot-pink chair."

Mommy said, "I understand. Your class classroom was very nice. What else do you miss about school?"

GiaBella thought for a moment and said, "I miss..."

"Snack time, with my friends Eva and Antonio."

"What was your favorite snack?"

GiaBella said with a big smile, "Chocolate chip cookies."

Mommy says, "Oh yes, snack time sounds like fun. What else do you miss?"

GiaBella gave it some thought. "I know..."

"I miss recess, because it is so much fun. Eva, Antonio and I would play catch and swing on the swing sets."

"Oh yes, recess is a lot of fun. Do you miss anyting else?"

GiaBella thought for a moment and said, "Yes, I miss going…"

"To the library and having story time."

Mommy said, "Story time sounds very nice. Is there anything else you miss?"

GiaBella thought for a moment and said, "Yes, I miss..."

"Gym, playing basketball with Eva and Antonio."

"Gym sounds like a lot of fun. Is there anything else you missed?"

GiaBella thought for just a little longer. "Oh yes, I miss my favorite Art class."

Mommy said, "Oh yes, art class is a lot of fun. Do you miss anything else?"

21

GiaBella thought for a moment and said, "Yes, I miss...science."

Mommy said, "Science is very interesting. GiaBella, now it is time to start your remote learning."

"Mommy, can I ask you a question?"

"Of course GiaBella, what would you like to ask me?"

"Mommy, when am I going to go back to school? Because..."

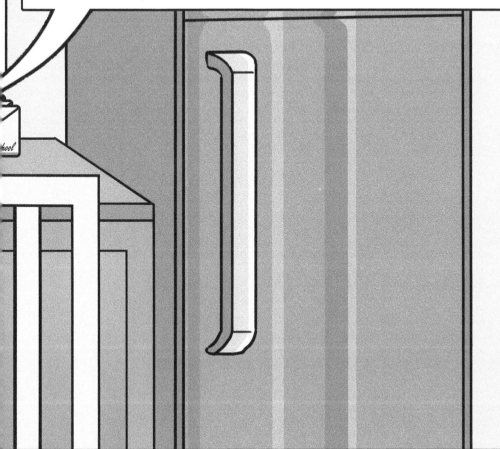

.

About the Author

The author's name is Michael Marinaccio. He has been married for ten years and a father of five children. When COVID-19 hit the New Jersey area in March of 2020, schools shut down until September 2020. He watched his daughter, GiaBella, doing her online classes at home one day a week. One afternoon after class, he asked her how she liked the online classes and she said, "I miss school." He asked her what she missed and

that is how he came up with the idea.
He felt that if GiaBella missed school,
then a lot of children must feel the
same way she does.

CPSIA information can be obtained
at www.ICGtesting.com
Printed in the USA
LVHW071316021121
702215LV00007B/122